For Erick (Duffy)

from

Aunt Melba and Uncle James

BILL COSBY

The Worst Day of My Life

by Bill Cosby

Illustrated by Varnette P. Honeywood

Introduction by Alvin F. Poussaint, M.D.

SCHOLASTIC INC.

New York   Toronto   London   Auckland   Sydney

Assistants to art production: Rick Schwab, Nick Naclerio

Library of Congress Cataloging-in-Publication Data

Cosby, Bill, 1937-
    The worst day of my life / by Bill Cosby; illustrated by Varnette P. Honeywood.
      p.   cm.— (Little Bill books for beginning readers)
    "Cartwheel books."
    Summary: Little Bill's parents expect him to dress up and act like a gentleman during their party, even though he would rather be playing soccer with his friends.
    ISBN 0-590-52175-6 (hardcover) 0-590-52190-X (pbk)
    [1. Behavior—Fiction.] I. Honeywood, Varnette P., ill. II. Title. III. Series: Cosby, Bill,
1937-   Little Bill books for beginning readers.
PZ7.C8185Wo   1999
[E] —dc21   98-53062
                                              CIP
                                             AC
10 9 8 7 6 5 4 3 2 1   9/9 0/0 01 02 03 04

Printed in the U.S.A.   23
First printing, September 1999

To Ennis,
"Hello, friend,"
B.C.

To the Cosby Family,
Ennis's perseverance against the odds
is an inspiration to us all,
V.P.H.

Dear Parent:

It's Saturday, but Little Bill won't be having any fun; his parents are giving a party. He has to get dressed up and spend time with a lot of adults he hardly knows, who will embarrass him by talking about how cute he used to be and how tall he's grown. Even a sociable child like Little Bill can become bored, or painfully shy, in such situations. Yet practicing social skills in various settings, with people of all ages, is important to a child's development.

Adult parties don't have to be unpleasant for children. Parents who sense that their kids might be uncomfortable can tell them ahead of time about the people they'll be meeting, talk about what they can expect, and listen to their concerns. (For very shy children, rehearsing a few sentences of small talk can be a real confidence booster.)

Some children take part eagerly if they're allowed to have a role in planning the event. Others enjoy acting as hosts and take pride in directing guests to the coat closet, serving food—even helping to clean up. It also makes a big difference to kids if they're allowed to take a play break after they've greeted the family's guests, and the benefit can be mutual, since adults usually want to have some conversations not meant for a child's ears.

When Little Bill's friends come by with a soccer ball, he surprises himself by not risking his good clothes (and his good behavior) to kick it around with them. Instead of acting on impulse and messing up, he chooses to honor his parents' wishes. So he tells his friends he can't play that day, and once he makes that responsible decision, he discovers that acting grown-up—at least for a while—can have its own rewards.

Alvin F. Poussaint, M.D.
Clinical Professor of Psychiatry,
Harvard Medical School and
Judge Baker Children's Center,
Boston, MA

Chapter One

It was Saturday. I was in the bathroom. I was standing at the sink. My mom was calling me. But I couldn't move my eyes.

I could hear the water running. I had the toothbrush and the toothpaste in my hands. But I couldn't move my eyes. Old people call that daydreaming.

My mother called me again. "Little Bill, let's move it."

But my body would not behave. I tried to open the toothpaste tube. But my fingers would not behave. The top of the tube fell and went down the drain. Nothing was behaving.

I tried to squirt some toothpaste. It made a popping sound and I had two splats of toothpaste—one on my toothbrush and one on my nose. Nothing was behaving.

As I brushed my teeth, I thought about how today I was supposed to play. But Mom and Dad had people coming over. I didn't know who they were, and I didn't know why they were coming over. I just know that when people come over, I can't go biking, I can't go swimming, I can't play soccer. I can't play! This was going to be the worst day of my life.

Why did *I* have to be there? Couldn't I just say hello and then leave? I bet if I said something not nice, my parents would send me to my room and I would get out of it. But then I'd just be in my room.

Chapter Two

My mom wanted me to wear my best clothes.

I searched my closet and found my favorite sweatpants. They had only one tiny hole in the knee. I couldn't find my best T-shirt in the closet, so I looked in the hamper. It was just a little wrinkled and it didn't smell bad.

While I was sniffing my shirt, Mom walked into my room.

"Those are not your best clothes," she said. "These are your best clothes."

She had a jacket, a shirt, a tie, and pants all on a hanger in one hand and a shiny pair of shoes in the other hand.

When I came out of my room, I could see that Mom and Dad were pleased with me. I was miserable.

"Why do I have to wear a tie? It's choking me," I said.

"You wear a tie to help you remember to be good" Dad laughed. "That's what ties are for. They are for reminding boys to be good."

I could tell that my parents were not going to let me take off the tie. So I tried the jacket.

"It's too hot. I think I'm going to faint," I said.

"The jacket stays on, too, Little Bill," my mother said.

"Why do I have to wear a jacket on such a warm day?" I asked.

"Because gentlemen wear jackets— even on warm days," said Mom.

The shoes were my last hope.

"Why do I have to wear these shoes?" I asked. "They make my feet feel trapped. And the soles are all slippy-slidey. I'll fall in them and get hurt."

"You won't fall in them because you won't run in them," said Dad. "These shoes are not for running. They are for sitting down and making polite conversation."

I made a grumpy face, but when I looked in the mirror, I had to admit that I looked really good.

Chapter Three

Our house was usually too neat and clean. Today it was neater and cleaner than ever. And the yard didn't even look like ours. There was a big tent with tables and fancy tablecloths and flowers.

"What happened to my badminton net?" I asked.

"It's safe inside the garage," said Mom.

"And what happened to my basketball hoop?" I asked. It was wrapped in ribbons and bows and had a balloon flying from it. "My basketball hoop is wearing a wedding dress!"

"Oh, dear!" Mom said to Dad. "Do you think I overdid it?"

Dad looked out the window.

"The basketball hoop looks beautiful," he said. He smiled. Then he started to hum... *"Here comes the bride...."*

Mom had to stop worrying about the basketball hoop because now she had something else to worry about. A parade of people carrying trays marched through our house and went out to the yard.

"Oh, dear, the food is already here," said Mom.

But it didn't look like food. It
looked like arts-and-crafts projects
made by a bunch of kindergartners.
And it didn't smell like food. I don't
know what it smelled like, but it
didn't smell like food.

Then the doorbell rang and
people came pouring in.

Chapter Four

I was trapped by Mom and two of her friends.

"How *are* you?" the man said to me.

But Mom wouldn't let me answer.

"He's fine," my mother said. "Tell Mr. Flum you're fine."

"Let the boy answer," said Mr. Flum.

"I'm fine," I said.

"My, how you've grown," said Mr. Flum.

"Do you know how tall you were the last time I saw you?" said Mrs. Flum.

I didn't remember the last time I saw her. I didn't even know who she was. Why do grown-ups ask such embarrassing questions? Kids don't do that.

"The last time I saw you, you were only this high." Mrs. Flum held her hand up to her knees. "And do you know what you did? Your mother was having a lovely party and I was talking to a very interesting man.

"All of a sudden, I felt someone grab my knees. It was you. I looked down to see that you were as surprised as I was. Your mother and I had been wearing the same color pants, and you thought I was she."

My parents' friends laughed and laughed. I didn't think that story was funny at all.

Mom and Mrs. Flum started to chat. That left me with Mr. Flum asking a whole lot of questions about school that I didn't want to answer.

As he spoke, I noticed that Mr. Flum had little hairs sticking out of his nose and more little hairs sticking out of his ears.

When I first looked at the guy, he looked normal. But the more I looked at his face, the more strange stuff I saw.

While Mr. Flum talked to me, I looked at the weird things on his face—a scar on his chin, a pimple near his nose, a mole under his eye.

"I can tell that you're a deep thinker by the way you're looking at me," said Mr. Flum. "So, what are you thinking, son?"

I looked over to where my mother was talking to the woman whose legs I had squeezed when I was little.

If I had told the truth, I would have made up a poem:

I was thinking about the hairs
That are growing out of your nose,
And wondering if they could grow
All the way down to your toes,
And cover your clothes.

But I didn't think Mom would want me to say that. And I didn't think Mr. Flum would want to hear that. So I just said, "Nothing."

Mr. Flum laughed, opening his mouth so wide I could see silver fillings in his teeth.

Then Mr. and Mrs. Flum said they were going to look at the canapés. I think that meant they were going to eat a whole lot of the arts-and-crafts food.

Chapter Five

If you know me, you know that this is the part of the story where I usually mess up.

I might have seen a cat and chased it and fell. I would have scuffed my shoes, ripped my pants, and dirtied my shirt. And then my mom would have said, "Little Bill, I need to speak to you in private," and I would have been in trouble.

But that's not what happened.

I might have been standing in front of the table with the arts-and-crafts food. I might have reached for one of the little crackers with the black, bubbly stuff on top, and knocked over the whole tray of crackers. I might have picked them up from the ground and put them back, and no one would have noticed that a little dirt had gotten on them.

Well, maybe someone would have noticed. And then my mom would have said, "Little Bill, I need to speak to you in private," and I would have been in trouble. But that's not what happened.

This is what happened.

I was getting tired of being around so many old people. So I walked to the front of my house to be alone for a while. At that moment, Andrew, José, and Kiku were coming toward my house. As they walked, they passed a soccer ball to each other.

"Hey, look at Little Bill," Andrew called. "Doesn't he look fine?"

"Over to you, Little Bill," José said. And he kicked the ball in my direction.

My toes were twitching and my legs were itching. All the muscles in my body were saying, "Kick the ball, Little Bill."

But I didn't.

I thought about how much my mom wanted me to be a gentleman and how my dad wanted me to be good. And I knew that my shoes were for making polite conversation and not for kicking soccer balls.

Most of the time, my parents let me do what I want to do. On this day, I would do what my parents wanted me to do. And do you know something? It wasn't the worst day of my life after all.

"You'll have to chase the ball yourself," I called. "I can't play today. I'll see you guys tomorrow."

I watched my friends until they turned a corner. Then I went back to my parents' party—to the table with the arts-and-crafts food.

A tall woman with short blonde hair put her hand on my shoulder. I had no idea who she was.

"Little Bill," she said, "you have really grown up."

She was right.

I popped a canapé into my mouth. And I didn't even drop any of the black, bubbly things on my tie!

Bill Cosby is one of America's best-loved storytellers, known for his work as a comedian, actor, and producer. His books for adults include *Fatherhood*, *Time Flies*, *Love and Marriage*, and *Childhood*. Mr. Cosby holds a doctoral degree in education from the University of Massachusetts.

Varnette P. Honeywood, a graduate of Spelman College and the University of Southern California, is a Los Angeles-based fine artist. Her work is included in many collections throughout the United States and Africa and has appeared on adult trade book jackets and in other books in the Little Bill series.